Existence

AN ODYSSEY THROUGH THE SEA OF INFATUATION, LOVE AND THE GRANDER THINGS

A COLLECTION OF POEMS

RT CHIWUTA

Illustrated by artspixels.com

Existence
An Odyssey Through The Sea Of Infatuation, Love And The Grander Things

Copyright © 2023 by RT Chiwuta
Illustrated by artspixels.com

Paperback ISBN: 978-1-63812-808-3
Ebook ISBN: 978-1-63812-809-0

All rights reserved. No part in this book may be produced and transmitted in any form or by any means, electronic, or mechanical, including photocopying, recording, or by any information storage and retrieval system, without permission in writing from the copyright owner.

The viThe views expressed in this work are solely those of the author and do not necessarily reflect the views of the publisher. It hereby disclaims any responsibility for them.

Published by Pen Culture Solutions 10/12/2023

Pen Culture Solutions
1-888-727-7204 (USA)
1-800-950-458 (Australia)
support@penculturesolutions.com

Existence
An exploration of the phenomenon of love

This book is dedicated to love. Love as the highest expression of being a human being. Most importantly, it is dedicated to love in the best way, in the most meaningful way. The book was inspired by romance. As the blossoming of an unexpected romance came and transformed existence all of a sudden out of a period that had been really challenging in my life.

So clearly again, the power of love became apparent. It's fine to theorise something, but to experience it and do it is another thing, to see it at work.

Love can be a nebulous thing like most things in our life. It's our obsession. However, I believe in it not only as a raison detre but as a belief system. Just as a religious person would believe on account of their religion, that's how I believe in love, without being religious about it.

The pursuit of it, the application of it and even the transcendent, higher dimensional, Universal and even God aspects of it.

However, without getting overly philosophical, this book is dedicated to the exploration of love between two people as a way of exploring the phenomenon of love. Then, consequently, hopefully through reading and exploring the book and the poems, the reader can come away with a deepened sense of love and ultimately its power and beauty.

That's the aim, point being, if most, if not all of the world believed in love with just a bit more awareness and devotion. That is to say, the highest appreciation of love, what kind of world would it be?

Hey listen, a man can dream right, postulate, offer my message. If that's what the universe has told me to do or write, who am I to deny. In any event, that's just to bring levity to what is otherwise a very serious proposal, supposition and hypothesis.

I believe a deep meditation on love for the human race would offer some kind of elixir. I have been writing away my human frustration since my early twenties. I am almost forty. To some extent more liberated from the constricting feelings of hatred, vengeance, anger, and all the rest of it. I realise though however that there is always room to grow and really I am probably a neophyte on this what I'm clear is a spiritual journey. However, my highest appreciation now is love. Its power, its deepest contemplation, its meaning.

So, what do we have in the world at the moment? Ukraine versus Russia. China versus America and all the rest of it and the sphere of influences and what they want to control. Africa and where it is, colonial history and neo colonialism, political transition or inflection point. The Middle East and its issues conflicts and divisions. Iran and the civil unrest there. Afghanistan and the Taliban taking over after Western occupation. South America with Bolsonaro and Lula Da Silva. The history of the United States in South America with the whole Monroe doctrine. We've just had or have Covid and its effect on us in every way, health wise, the world economy, conflict between so called Covid deniers and the mainstream view. Climate crisis as it's called. Migration or immigration issues. Exploitation. Culture wars, transgenderism and just personal life and struggles.

So why not meditate on love? I believe in hope and even at my lowest and darkest times in my life I still had hope. Even when I was close to the edge, love brought me back from the edge. I have so many things to love and have been showered by love in my life. As a result, I believe through discovering love, as a tool, collectively, humanity can truly discover something for itself. Work through its struggles and differences instead of fighting. How novel would that be? Or at least it's just an idea.

In any case, don't let me stop you .....

EXISTENCE

Hope and possibility,
The engine for all that's possible,
When one always connects,
And is connected to their hopes and possibility,
They are indestructible,
Indefatigable,
Can remain unbroken to the myriad forces that pervade existence and come to break the will,
Test the will,
And at times the will,
Will be broken,
But hope and the believe in possibility,
Even in impossible times,
Is that spark,
That oxygen,
That creates life even in the vacuum of despair,
So never lose hope,
And always believe in the possibility of everything you wish for,
Everything you imagine being possible.

Life can be a place of solitude at times,
But it's in the solitude where you can,
If you listen,
Hear God whisper to us,
Only gently,
Just to say you're not alone,
You're never alone,
You are always surrounded by the infinity of all that is,
The love of God,
And every upset is just a test,
A challenge ,
A point in the journey,
To guide you towards the only answer,
And that answer is true love,
And that's only if you are in the awareness,
The awareness that,
All we are doing here,
Is working our way back to true love,
And the only way to truly appreciate it,
The only way to grow,
Is at times to feel or be disconnected from it,
But the truth is,
You are never disconnected,
That's just the illusion that brings this life to reality,
God is love,
God is true,
God is everywhere,
God is always there,
Especially in the worst moments,
They are only a passing phase,
Life is a passing phase,
And relative to the length of infinity,
The suffering we experience here,
Well,
It's so short lived,
It might as well have never happened,

EXISTENCE

But of course it does happen,
At least in our perception of reality,
Our experience of reality,
And that's our life,
So know that God is always with you,
In every moment eternal love exists,
Even when you are wronged,
That's eternal love,
An opportunity to find the good in yourself,
Your center,
To activate your faculties of love and understanding,
For how can you know what love is if you never experience hate,
Or what patience is if you never experience anger,
Without the challenges there is no life,
And sometimes in the misery we ask why God?
But know God sees all,
Knows all,
Watches over all,
And like a truly loving parent,
Even as they scold,
It's for your greater good.

I have observed with careful intrigue,
This woman who's appeared from the blue,
Curious about the course of destiny,
What strange tricks the universe can play,
Catch you off guard,
A surprise,
A bit of magic,
That's why it's wise to live in the wonder,
Live in hope,
Always carry optimism,
Even in the darkest times,
Especially in the darkest times,
For you never know what beauty lies round the corner.

EXISTENCE

The warrior princess,
Strong and powerful,
Like the fabled amazons,
Like the Agojie of the Dahomey,
Fierce and driven,
Battle hardened like an axe,
But soft and sensitive like a rose petal,
Won't settle for the mediocrity of life,
Will only accept the best,
Knows her true worth,
Knows her true value,
Beautiful,
Buxom,
Voluptuous,
A true woman,
The warrior princess.

Out of the blue she came,
When loneliness and solitude had become such an acquaintance they hurt no more,
Full of fun,
Full of jokes,
Full of wit and grit,
In the most unexpected way,
At the most unexpected time,
But right on time,
Like the most elaborate cosmic plan,
That when great dramas and events that derail and confound had subsided,
And all of a sudden there was a space for something new,
A friend arrived,
Just on time,
Like it had all been planned all along,
How sweet it is,
To live in hope for good things,
And how sweeter still,
When they happen.

EXISTENCE

She is a queen,
With or without a crown,
Regal,
Royal,
Resplendent,
Beautiful,
Inside and out,
Affable,
Yet serious when it matters,
The balance of the universe flows within her,
An African Queen,
A queen.

Valentine's day,
A day that's been dedicated for love,
For lovers,
For the pursuit of love,
To honour love,
But In this day when at times the true meaning of things is lost in commercialism,
One sided expectation,
Cheap thrills that don't last long,
Maybe valentine's day can be a crucial day,
A day we truly reflect on what love is,
And what one person can truly mean to another,
And what love is in this ever changing world,
However there seems to be something special to this poet,
Something unique about meeting that one person,
Dedicating your life to them,
Your soul and commitment,
To sacrifice the temptation of everything else in pursuit of a unique bond,
A unique understanding,
A unique connection,
It seems a noble quest,
And perhaps the hardest to achieve,
Perhaps that's why it's the pinnacle of the lover's pursuit,
Hence, on valentine's day,
Maybe the secret is not to buy the biggest bunch of roses,
As nice as that is,
As good as that is,
And perhaps even as appropriate as that is,
Maybe the secret is to contemplate on what true love really is.

EXISTENCE

Life is beautiful,
Especially in the moments of sadness,
Even in the deepest sadness,
For all it is preparing us for,
Is the greatest ecstasy,
Whether it's in this life or the next,
No matter how long it takes,
Ode on a sad day.

19/02/2023

Truly authentic experiences are very rare in this life,
Thank you for giving me a truly authentic experience,
Thank you for opening up to me,
Being vulnerable,
And being sensitive,
Excellent and incredible characteristics,
Also good fun and light hearted,
I learnt you are strong and resilient,
Adaptable and a born survivor,
A true adventurer with a fearless spirit,
It is truly inspiring and moving,
When you see a human being with your eyes you see the body,
But when you get to know them and speak to them in their depth,
A whole new universe opens up,
Thank you for opening up to me and giving me the privilege to spend time with you.

EXISTENCE

As the early embers of love bristle,
Like new coals being put in a kiln,
Firing up the engines of life,
The steam train of possibility,
New found love ignites all,
Like a dazzling firework display,
Or a rush of comets in the sky,
A moment in time of great possibility,
Everything is lit up,
Enlivened,
A flame of possibility,
The only question then is to keep that flame burning,
Like the Olympic flame,
Which should never extinguish,
As long as the games are still running,
The game of life,
So then, how do we keep new found love burning?
It seems the art is not to let it light up and burn too bright,
Lest it burns out really quickly as it uses up all its fuel,
But to nurse it,
To blow on it,
Caress it,
Nurture it,
Tenderly,
Caringly,
Carefully,
Like how they made fire with flint before the match,
Carefully and skilfully,
It didn't start as a mighty flame,
It started with careful intention,
And a spark,
Eventually it would grow into a mighty flame,
So maybe we should learn from them,
Learn from that,
That we are falling in love the wrong way,

Swept up in a mighty blaze of passion and ecstasy at the beginning which then ebbs away,
When it should maybe start as a slow careful flame built with purpose intention and patience,
Then you feed more and more and wood,
Till it's a sustaining comforting fire that brings warmth to all,
And burns,
And burns,
And burns,

EXISTENCE

If you are love,
Then the whole world is love,
The whole universe is love,
If only love exists in you,
Then only love exists out there,
That is the exchange,
What you are,
What you believe,
Is what everything is out there,
So if you are love,
Then everything is love.

Love,
We keep getting tested,
Because we need to keep growing,
Sometimes we think we've found the answer,
Finally,
All the questions have been answered,
I've found all the meaning,
All the reason for the suffering,
Then more misery comes in the space,
Then we are left perplexed,
Flummoxed,
But I thought that was it,
I thought this was it,
That's because though we need to keep growing,
We are here to grow,
Relative to the span of time,
Our time here is but a blip,
To experience the whole gamut of what there is to experience,
And we experience the most,
When we feel the most,
That's the exchange,
That's why the most pain,
Brings the most growth and understanding,
If you are willing to grow,
In this life at least,
The main thing is to be committed to growth,
Upward learning,
Through love,
Through it all.

EXISTENCE

The greatest epiphany is love,
The loving space,
And the greatest reality is having love in your heart and in your mind,
For if it's just in the heart,
Then the mind,
The brain can corrupt it,
As the brain looks to cope with the nature of our reality,
The limitations of our reality,
The challenges of our reality,
The limitations of our cognitive perceptions,
Social and existential conditionings,
Supposed reason and logic,
So called cold calculations,
Which force us to kill at times, be selfish and vindictive,
Hateful,
Spiteful,
But if love exists both in your heart as a phenomenon,
And in your mind,
Your brain,
As a raison detre,
A concept,
An algorithm,
As you would understand complex mathematics,
Your brain understands the complex algebra of love,
As pertains this life,
Then that's a truly powerful force,
Then the heart beats and enlightens a way,
And the brain calculates and navigates the right path through life's problems,
Through love,

When you heart starts to sink from a broken heart,
Let it,
Let it,
Let it,
As you start to feel as though you are descending into an abyss,
A vortex of pain,
The first and greatest lesson is to know that everything especially here is ephemeral,
All our pain is short lived,
Even if it lasts a life time,
And if it lasts for a life time,
Then what you had to learn here was greater or truly great,
So as the heart sinks from a broken heart,
Let it,
Let it go right to the bottom,
But then try not to be lost to vices and distractions,
Try as is humanly possible,
Instead look to learn,
To feel,
To connect,
With the light,
The good things,
Of course love,
Indeed Love,
Those are the good things,
And when you reach the bottom of the abyss of the broken heart,
If you have taken love with you down there,
Then upon when you rise back up,
Your whole being is love,
Right from the pit of your woes and dark shadows,
To the most elevated parts of yourself.

EXISTENCE

The path of true love,
Is to walk the highest path,
Make the most sacrifices,
Have the most understanding,
Have the highest ideals,
Have the most meaningful intention,
Have the deepest wisdom,
The greatest clarity of thought,
Life confounds,
Perhaps its meant to confound,
Make what should be clear unclear,
Make the right path as tortuous as possible,
Perhaps that's why true accomplishment is a windy path,
But as the most perfect blade is forged in extreme heat,
So the path of true love can be like a furnace,
Unceasing challenges,
When you think the storms have gone,
The confusion has calmed down,
New storms come,
And new things to figure out,
But life is active and dynamic,
And we must continuously evolve,
Evolve upwards,
And that is the path of true love,
The endless Upward path to your better self,
The best self you can possibly be,
Despite the worst of yourself you might have seen.

Being able to love,
Also means being able to hate,
Hence, being able to really love,
Can also mean being able to truly hate,
Great risk and shadows lie at the heart of this duality,
Care and caution in these treacherous waters.
This is the human condition,
The condition of our existence.

EXISTENCE

To risk it all for love,
Again and again,
Even after great heartbreak and pain,
Is an act of courage,
The Dilemma though is not to carry the scars of battles past,
But the lessons,
To not seek new love out of desperation,
But rather to fulfil on the purpose of love,
For to love wholly you have to be whole yourself,
Then love is just an expression of affinity for another,
Not a band aid over great holes and deficiencies,
That kind of love can constrict and control,
Maybe even torture,
Torture the soul,
So the path of love can be a courageous one,
Especially after great loss or pain when you've really loved,
But if you are truly walking the path of love,
Of true love,
Then it's good to love again,
Seek it out again,
Believe in it again.

Then the sun shines again,
Even more brighter,
And perhaps not brighter,
But more splendidly,
For a splendid sun,
Is different to a bright sun,
A bright sun illuminates,
Which is good,
But a splendid sun ignites the imagination,
Arouses the emotions,
Deep emotions,
So when it's been dark,
And you've been trapped in darkness,
How splendid it is,
To awaken to a splendid sun.

EXISTENCE

What purpose it is to have someone to love,
Something to love,
A raison detre,
Something to wake up for,
To drive you,
Inspire passion,
Give you purpose,
What purpose.

Now it's grown up straight talk,
In the dark arts of love,
Perhaps to begin with games is necessary and acceptable to begin with,
Flirting,
Denial,
Persuasion,
The chase,
Ferreting out the deepest intention,
But in the end it becomes about straight honest hard talk,
Especially in later life,
When so much is in the space,
Experiences,
Good, bad and horrible,
At that point then,
Games are for children and liars,
But real lovers speak the truth to each other,
Those truly pursuing it,
Then it becomes a choice,
Whether to climb the totem pole of love,
To go up, up and up,
To the dizzying heights of ecstatic love and connection,
Self-actualisation,
Spiritual bliss,
Or remain a mere mortal.

EXISTENCE

To love with the intensity of a million suns,
A love that burns ever brighter,
Burns right in the center of your heart,
Such that if one sun was to fade after a billion years,
There would be many more left in its stead,
The love of all love,
A million,
Billion,
Trillion years,
To infinity,
That's the love I dream of.

You see,
The thing about true love,
Is it's not about physical beauty,
Though attraction is an aid,
Physical attraction is only truly real when there's mental attraction,
This is in the case of love,
And not lust,
More so true love,
Because when it's just lust,
That physical attraction can pass if the mental attraction fades,
And that's just our base instincts,
Atavism,
Hence, when you truly love,
It transcends the physical,
You observe the being,
As though from a higher plain,
Where beauty means more than morphology and dimples,
Your observation then becomes,
Personal,
Transcendent,
Enhanced and spiritual,
Hence why they say,
Beauty lies in the eyes of the beholder,
They see with their real eyes,
The eyes of the soul,
The eyes of inner wisdom,
Which see deeper,
And truer,
That's why even in old age,
When the skin is wrinkled,
The skin sags,
The body is brittle and broken,
Hunched over like the hunch back of Notre dame,
You can look at your loved one,
And see the most beautiful thing that ever existed.

EXISTENCE

Love is like the unfurling of a flower,
The blossoming a flower,
To reveal the beautiful colours,
From a hard pod,
All of a sudden you see the soft petals,
Soft and tender,
Soft bright coloured petals,
And nectar to be found within,
For the bees to go and make their honey,
So love is like an opportunity for sweetness,
The sweetest things,
Nature guides and shows in her own way,
Lessons to learn,
About deeper wisdoms,
Deeper insights,
So as the blossoming of a flower,
Leads to sweet sweet honey,
So the blossoming of love,
Can lead to sweet sweet things,
The sweetest of things.

The center of a person's heart,
The center of a loving person's heart,
Their inner core,
Their inner sanctum,
Is like a secret garden,
Where nymphs, fairies and beautiful creatures live,
A little magical sanctum,
Where one can get lost in all that's beautiful,
All that's magical,
So if you can find it,
What a special place it can be.

EXISTENCE

True love,
Comes and makes what was already complete,
Complete,
What was already whole,
Whole,
What was already beautiful,
Beautiful,
True love elevates,
Enhances,
Accentuates,
In a more incredible way,
True love comes and makes what was already incredible,
More incredible,
So if you want true love,
Be all those things above,
And you will have it,
Because if you're broken,
That true love can't grow,
Like seeds in a barren field,
Or a field full of thorns,
The most beautiful garden will grow in the richest soil,
And be grown by the perfect gardener,
So know and accept you're whole complete and perfect,
Worthy of true love,
And True love will come to you.

Your love is like the sunshine and the moonlight,
It illuminates both the night and day,
Your beauty,
Your truth,
Illuminates both the light and the dark,
Enhances the light in me,
Diminishes and exposes my dark shadows,
This is beyond a precious gift,
It's heavenly,
It's God sent.

EXISTENCE

To love,
As in when you make a stand for something,
Draw a line in the sand,
Make a declaration,
Devote yourself to something,
Something bigger,
Something greater than yourself,
Something that will leave a mark,
A legacy ,
Make a change,
Have a meaningful impact,
A positive transformation,
To love such that you're called to action,
Against a great foe,
For a great cause,
To achieve something special,
Something generational,
Inter-generational,
Multi-generational,
Something Transcendent,
That's the power of love.

Love shouldn't be about need,
Or expectation,
In the strictest sense,
Synergy springs more to mind,
Synergy creates a greater whole,
A greater outcome,
From independent separate entities.

EXISTENCE

Time is a relative construct,
And in the human realm,
It is linear,
Tick tock,
Tick tock,
However,
With regards to emotions,
The reality is they are fluid,
Transcendent,
And outside of the phenomenon of time,
Time as we perceive it,
So as humans,
We believe love should occur after a more elapsed period,
Romantic love anyway,
But in reality,
At times,
It can be instantaneous,
Love at first sight they say,
Telling us more about our connection to each other,
About the overwhelming,
Over aweing power of love.

I love you like my heart is about to explode,
But I can't let it explode,
Because I need it to live,
A love that's like a bridge between what's possible,
And what's impossible,
A love that bridges the gap between what you thought could never happen,
But is happening,
A reality that you didn't know could be,
But is occurring,
That's how much I love you,
Like a whole new paradigm,
I love you because you inspire strength, courage and vulnerability,
At the same time a sense of invulnerability,
I love you as someone who's loved before,
And thought they knew love,
What it was,
What it could be,
What it should be,
But alas they were a tenderfoot,
Perhaps a hapless romantic,
But this is transcendent,
Real,
So real you can touch it.

EXISTENCE

So in the end,
Life is just a game,
Just a test,
A paradigm,
A plain,
Rigged with tricks and twists,
All an elaborate ruse,
To teach the soul,
To find its way to true love.

I miss you today,
And I'm sad,
I'm not sad because I'm heart broken and life is not going well,
I'm sad because I'm not next to you,
And since I met you,
Life has so much potential all of a sudden,
Even though it did before,
It has more so now that you are here,
So I'm also sad because I'm fearful,
That what if something gets in the way,
But to live in fear is to surrender to the darkness,
You must live with positive expectation,
In all circumstances,
And if life seemingly puts a real wrench in the gears of your existence,
Know that everything is ephemeral in this plain,
And all you must do is grow more, more and more,
The greater the pain,
The greater the epiphany when you get out the other side,
In this life or the next.

EXISTENCE

I love you because your love is like a lighthouse,
It guides me home,
Like a ship to shore,
I love you,
Because just like the light of a light house,
Your love lights the way,
Guides the way,
From the rocks,
That would sink a ship if it got too close to them,
And lose all its precious cargo,
Even in a storm,
The right path to take is illuminated,
And just like the light of a light house,
Your love arrived just in time,
To point the way to the true destination,
Where I can set my anchor,
From the long windy voyage,
It feels as though I can rest now,
For I'm finally home.

The kind of love,
Such that,
If you lost it all,
All you had built,
Had crumbled to ruin,
And all you had left in your possession,
Was a cardboard box,
And you were sitting under it,
In the rain,
You would still be happy,
Because you are with the one you love,
That kind of love.

EXISTENCE

To love without attachment or concern,
The purest space for expression,
Attachment and concern,
Can induce fear,
And fear can get in the way,
So to love free of these,
Is the way to really love,
Just love,
Just for the phenomenon of it.

To transcend the earthly plain,
And be in the higher realms of divinity,
Higher realms of consciousness,
Higher levels of awakened awareness,
Higher levels of appreciation of it all,
Whilst in the paradigm of this dimension,
The gift of pure love,
Trans portative love,
Transcendent love,
A devotion to love,
When you truly love,
You see,
You can see it all,
You can see through the mess,
As bewildering as it is,
Then one day you're above it all,
Perhaps floating peacefully and harmlessly,
Like a cirrus cloud on a hot summer day,
Just an incidental phenomenon of no real consequence,
Part of it all,
But free from it all,
The freeing power of love,
When you see it all,
When you really see it all.

EXISTENCE

Somehow,
Somewhere along the line,
We were sold this idea of the one,
The one true love,
And yet it seems so elusive,
Marriages don't seem to last,
And the ones that do,
Some it's because breaking up is seen as harder,
And in days gone by it was a taboo,
Marriage was for life,
And in some places still,
And in a world of so many billions,
How can you meet this one?
What if you live in a small village?
Your culture won't allow you to marry outside of it?
All these extraneous variables,
Is this idea a myth?
Just a legend?
Just a mythological tale created to arouse a belief in a phenomenon that does not exist?
Worse yet,
Sometimes you think you've find the so called one,
Then it turns out you haven't,
Suffer all the heart break that can cause,
And maybe never even recover from it,
So what is the real truth then?
What of polygamy?
Polyamory?
Because of course you can love many people,
Be attracted to many people,
So who said you should love just one?
Yet I dare to say there seems something uniquely special in finding that one,
Creating a unique special bond,
Better yet,
Trying,

And failing,
And trying again,
As a child who learns to walk,
They don't stop because they fell,
Or someone in the pursuit of mastery,
For the real lesson,
Is in life you never stop learning,
And then it's to say,
Even after multiple heartaches,
Perhaps even on the 1st attempt,
Imagine how special it is,
To find that one,
I believe it's a beautiful dream,
And to pursue absolute beauty,
As in the beauty of a loving relationship,
Well that's a truly good thing,
And better yet,
To really find the mythological one,
Yet as well,
To each their own,
That's the fairest position of a fair man,
Reality occurs differently for us all.

EXISTENCE

Losing your love,
Would be like losing the sun,
Everything would die,
The world would freeze over,
No life,
No warmth,
Reality just wouldn't be the same anymore,
The strange thing about falling deeply in love,
Is how someone who you didn't know not too long ago,
Now has so much meaning to your existence,
So much resonance,
So much importance to your life,
I guess that's why they call it falling in love,
For you do fall in,
Like you trip over,
Find yourself head over heels,
All of a sudden in a tail spin,
Upside down,
What fascinating creatures we are,
How fascinating this life.

How good it is to be in love,
When both are peace makers,
Yes of course,
Peace is the way,
Just as in broader life,
But yes in love,
Better yet if both are romantics,
Then the sky is the limit,
The possibility of what's possible is endless,
An Upward spiral staircase into the heavens,
Cloud nine as they call it,
In love,
Peace,
Romance,
And the spiral staircase to heaven.

EXISTENCE

To feel,
Is a gift from God,
Indeed the opportunity to feel is a gift from God,
A gift from the universe,
A gift from creation,
The creative force of life,
Especially to feel love,
Love for a loved one,
A close friend,
A child,
A lover,
A pet,
Indescribable a phenomenon,
Sometimes so beautiful it overwhelms,
So beautiful it comforts,
So beautiful it moves,
How kind it is to have been created?
So we could get an opportunity to feel,
Even more so to feel love,
Furthermore,
Love answers all,
It really does,
You want to be happy?
Love,
You want to feel peace?
Love,
You want to grow more as a person?
Learn to feel love more deeply,
Explore it's deeper dimensions,
Only a loving God could create so we could experience this,
When we might not have existed,
A truly loving God,
For the truth of it,
And what we don't see,
Is everything we go through that we say causes us pain,
Is an opportunity for us,

A gateway on the path to finding true love,
So when you find yourself not on the path of love,
The path of true love,
Of course life hurts,
Of course to get to the point of loving awareness is a journey,
But when you get there,
Oh what beauty every minute and second can be,
Despite what's happening,
So thank you God,
Thank you Universe,
For the opportunity to live,
The opportunity to love,
So to the individual I say,
Run for it,
Explore it,
Pursue the deepest meaning of life,
It is truly like digging for gold,
Spiritual gold,
Only this is the most precious gold,
That leads to actual true happiness.

EXISTENCE

A life of constant denial is boring,
I assert that this life is also to be enjoyed,
And yet a life of discipline is constructive,
So they say,
Everything in moderation,
So a treat here and there,
Let loose a little bit,
Be open minded,
But within a code and structure of strict discipline,
So in love,
Yes you can be free,
Let loose,
But within those protective bounds of a uniting commitment.

Then life begins,
The real test of your love,
The real test,
Is it infatuation?
Or is it real?
Are you willing to face and traverse challenges?
Or was it just a wave of emotion?
When the fantasy and dream,
Is brought crushing down by raw reality,
And yes that's reality,
The great gap between what we hope for at times,
And what is,
And more importantly what transpires,
How that plays out,
That becomes the story of your life,
The story of your love,
The story of your commitment,
Nothing is perfect so to speak in this realm,
And if it was,
There would be nothing to learn,
Nothing to do,
It would all be a static steady state,
It's in the apparent chaos of our life that this reality can be,
The truth is though,
It already is perfect,
Always will be,
So when you are misdirected,
You know,
All is perfect,
Just reorient,
Take a deep breath,
And keep learning,
Keep growing,
And most importantly,
Keep loving.

EXISTENCE

It's like a volcanic eruption,
A supernova,
An earthquake,
A tsunami,
A hurricane,
A big bang,
A life changing,
Reality shifting,
Landscape altering phenomenon,
When the overwhelming,
Undeniable,
Awe inspiring,
Other worldly,
Uncontrollable,
Snow ball effect,
Feeling of falling deeply in love takes over,
Things will just never be the same again.

Love is like a reference point for the human condition,
A compass of a sort,
An unmoving point in the ground which will always be there,
No matter how much you get lost,
We are meant to be confused at time whilst we are here,
Beguiled and bewildered,
Hurt and betrayed,
Robbed, beaten and worse,
To be disappointed and be in despair,
A sea of constant suffering at times,
In every direction,
Why?
Well that's for another Ode,
Another time,
But in this ode,
It's to say,
In all of that,
Love is the reference point,
The point where we build all hopes and aspirations,
Dreams and expectations,
Humanity's glue,
So when we are being forced apart,
Pulled to different poles,
All it is really is a call to discover the deeper aspects of love,
Dig deeper into our humanity,
And that's all there is really,
Then in that way a new space is open,
Then we see what there is to discover,
In this strange journey of ours.

EXISTENCE

It's ten days till we meet again,
It feels like a decade away,
I guess Einstein was of course right when he spoke about the relativity of time,
Certainly under certain conditions,
The manifestation of it changes,
And that's definitely true for us humans,
And it definitely feels true for me right now,
For these ten days,
Feel like a decade away,
How will I manage?
I can only but learn to be patient,
Although we've met already,
It somehow feels like we'll be meeting for the first time,
And this time when we meet,
Life will never be the same again,
Initially when we met,
We got acquainted,
And it was a beautiful acquaintance,
And in our time together,
You opened the door to my heart,
However it feels,
This time when we meet,
In the ten days which feel a decade away,
You will step inside the door,
And I will certainly let you in,
And hopefully you will make a home inside my heart forever,
That is my fondest wish,
Forever indeed,
For time is relative,
And the sort of love I hope for,
Goes beyond time,
It lasts forever.

I woke up today,
Before the sun rose,
Only to find out,
It's still nine whole days to go till we meet,
And it truly hit home,
That time for us is sequential,
We live moment to moment,
Moment by moment,
Second by second,
And there's nothing else we can do,
We can't jump forward or backwards,
This brings order and reliability to our universe,
Our existence,
Though our emotions may deceive us,
Our perceptions,
Make time feel like it's moving faster at times,
And deathly slow at others,
In the end,
In reality as it were,
It's a consistent, constant and unchanging,
Tick, tock,
A constant rhythm,
Like a universal discipline,
Tempering our spirits,
The wild storms that rage within us,
That sweep us off our feet in the tempest of life,
Providing a framework,
A structure for us to exist,
So, as I long for the time to elapse,
And by some miracle,
It's time for us to meet already,
In the next ten minutes,
And not the many minutes in the nine days to come,
I realise that perhaps it's an opportunity for a higher mastery,
The innumerable lessons your soul has already taught mine in such a short space of time,

EXISTENCE

Such as love is a rescuer,
Love is the answer,
Love is the guide,
Love builds and not destroys,
Love creates possibility for beautiful things,
Hate creates possibility for ugly things,
I realise that if I take a deep breath,
And bide my time,
And master the patience it's going to take to wait these nine days,
I will be a greater man,
For you,
And maybe for other things,
And so it is,
That you are here to build me up and I you,
And that is the message of true love,
So yes with positive anticipation ,
I see now that these 9 days,
Only mean I'll be on cloud 9,
When I finally get the honour to be in your presence.

Love is like an older brother,
A loving older brother,
The most loving old brother,
Who has always been there from the start,
Has always been your champion,
In the naivety of your youth,
He was your champion,
Standing up for you,
Standing instead of you,
Shielding you,
Always,
Most importantly,
When you thought it wasn't there,
The love,
It was there,
It was always there,
Because it was there where you needed it,
Always there in your hour of need,
Standing up to bullies,
The biggest bullies,
The scariest ones,
The ones everyone feared,
Not because he wasn't afraid,
But fear was arrested immediately as the bully went after his little brother,
So love conquers fear,
Love conquers the darkness,
Love inspires courage when courage is called upon,
I woke in tears from a dream,
As I dreamt that I was in a warm embrace with my older brother,
My shield,
My protector,
My ever present protector,
Our love transcended this realm into the next,
For in the dream,
I had feared losing him,

EXISTENCE

And I fought to keep him alive,
But when we embraced in the dream,
I realised he would always be with me,
And I cried tears in the waking realm,
And in the realm beyond our wakened state,
Thats real, real love.
Eight more days till I see you,
There is something symmetrical about the number eight,
Two circles,
One on top of the other,
I hear the mystics talk of sacred geometry,
Sacred mathematics,
Astrological timing,
I know nothing of these things,
But I certainly know that there was something sacred about how we met,
Sacred in the timing and your placement at this time period in my life,
Your seeming profoundness,
I choose not to dig too deeply into the mysterious,
I just deep my curious toe,
Just get a taste,
Like a wine taster who only sips to savour the taste,
But not get lost in the intoxication,
I only dip my toe,
For there is too much to know anyway,
So, to invest too much time in one thing,
Is to neglect all the other things,
So I choose to be in the guidance of the universe,
Though I know of sacred geometry,
Sacred mathematics,
And astrological phenomena,
I know nothing of it,
But I know all that was at play somehow,
And God,
The master script writer,

Wrote a beautiful script,
That brought you in my life,
So I could be amazed at the serendipity,
Like the most thrilling movie,
With the most incredible adventure,
Twist and turns,
This is Life for me,
And I contemplate this,
With eight days to go.

EXISTENCE

It's seven days now,
A so called week,
Somehow sounds better than ten days,
It's strange to describe this feeling,
Of tension,
Longing and impatience,
Perhaps it's the confluence of so many things,
Passionate, deep seated feelings,
An anxiety that this could be the one,
But the failure of past experiences haunt the space,
Like an angry ghost,
Seeking to destroy new possibilities,
A symptom of trying to find love after heartbreak, pain and disappointment,
Especially for the idealist romantic,
But they say you only fail when you give up,
So you should only give up when you're dead,
That way you never gave up,
You just expired,
And in that way you were never overcome,
A true force of nature and belief,
And in this case its belief in the highest power,
The most beautiful thing,
Love,
So it's seven days,
And as I navigate my near 4 decades of existence that have lead me to you now at this point,
That's almost half a life time,
I want this to be right,
The last love,
The one,
As it should have always been,
Right from the start,
From the days of youth and innocence,
Before life plotted its own windy bifurcated path,
And brought joy and despair,

Lessons and gains,
But now I seek peace and serenity,
For at its pinnacle,
That's what love produces,
Peace and serenity,
So seven more days to meditate,
Seven more days to anticipate,
Seven more days to live in imagination,
Before imagination becomes reality.

EXISTENCE

Six days.
To be the most unique.
You must go through the most unique challenges,
And if you can overcome them,
Then you wake up,
And inhabit a completely different reality,
When things don't go your way,
Life throws you a curve ball,
Or challenges you uniquely,
It's a request from the Universe,
Are you willing to bring out the special qualities in you?
In the best way,
As in the art of pugilism or even that dastardly thing,
War,
It's when victory is grabbed from the jaws of defeat,
When you win when eventualities have gone against you,
And you find that special spark,
Then a legend is born.

Five more days to go,
And the question really is becoming apparent,
Whether to love for a reason?
Or to love something?
Love for a purpose?
Love because you get something back?
Love because you belong?
Or love because that thing matters to you?
Like your child,
Your precious child,
Your mother,
Your father,
Your grand father,
Your friend,
Your best friend,
Your neighbourhood,
Your area,
Your region,
Your country,
Your continent,
Your race,
Your politics,
Your religion,
Your culture,
And everything else that we say we love,
Or then call love,
To love for that,
Or just love?
Just be love?
To all things,
To be the expression of it,
The embodiment of it,
Is that something humanely possible?
To imagine if we were just the spontaneous and ongoing expression of love,
In all meaningful ways,

EXISTENCE

Not as a romantic unattainable idealistic fantasy,
But somehow some functional matrix,
Some functional paradigm,
Based on everything it is to be human,
But somehow different,
Somehow new,
Somehow not what we have known,
What we have called love,
Still human,
But somehow the truth,
Of what true love is,
The same economics somehow,
Relationships,
Interdependence,
Maybe even politics,
But somehow different,
Different in all the best ways,
A new dimension of reality,
Imagined on the 5th day of anticipation

On the 4th day,
The idealism of love is brought into question,
Love often disappoints and brings great pain,
Romances fail all the time,
And always start with so much promise and seeming serendipity,
Abuse in relationships,
Power struggles,
Forced or arranged marriages where love isn't necessarily the question,
Not to say arranged marriages are wrong or bad in a sense,
Just that the efficacy or utility of the supposed partnership is seen as more important,
Though of course a loving bond can grow in this scenario,
Love can also cause extreme pain,
Not just in the loss or failure of a relationship,
But just to imagine the loss of a child,
Your parents,
The thought is unbearable,
The reality even more so,
You love them so much,
That losing them causes in some instances pain that lasts a life time,
So what's the point of loving?
Connecting,
Hoping,
Wishing,
Believing,
Only to be let down,
Only to lose dearly,
Only to be hurt deeply,
Excruciatingly,
Love drives others to insanity,
Like Hitler,
Loved his Germany so much he was razing the whole world,
Loved the vision of his great Aryan race,
A master race,

EXISTENCE

White supremacists and their love for their white skin,
Jihadists and their dream of a global Caliphate,
The Great British Empire,
The Roman Empire,
The Mongolian Empire and all the rest,
And to some lesser but just as relatively problematic extent,
Rabid nationalists,
Jingoists,
And even just nationalists,
They love their country,
Their land,
It's the best country in the world,
USA, USA, USA, USA,
The popular refrain,
Communist China,
It's all love,
Mother Russia,
Rule Brittania and all the rest of it,
People like to look at Hitler and say it was hate,
Yes you cannot say it was not,
But it was also love,
He Loved his country so much and his perfect Aryans,
He wanted to make them great and ubiquitous throughout the world,
The colonialists,
They did it for the love of their country and their race,
For Queen and Country,
Great acts of evil and tyranny,
And to this day they have a lot of pride in what they did,
I suppose conquest is enjoyable,
It's the defeated that weep,
To the winner the spoils,
We speak in laudable terms of the great conquerors of the past,
Napoleon Bonaparte,
Genghis Khan,
Shaka the Zulu,

William the Conqueror and the rest,
Who in reality were all brutal murderers,
We admire war and the supposed great generals,
Like the all admired General Robert E Lee in the American South,
I suppose just as the hunter goes to hunt to feed his children,
Every living being that hunts another to survive,
Does so for its off spring,
It's ultimately an expression of love,
So we kill really because we love,
Even all the corrupt leaders we cry about,
That steal from the nation,
They steal for the love of their children,
Their families,
Themselves,
They love themselves at the expense of everyone else,
So after expounding on the plaudits of love for all the preceding poems,
What now?
I don't know,
Maybe it's time to sleep,
It's almost one in the morning,
Perhaps it's a realisation for another day.

EXISTENCE

The irony of it,
Or at least the reality of it,
Reality in any case being a strange and nebulous word,
A strange and nebulous phenomenon,
So perhaps one can say,
Reality for us,
Reality for the individual,
Reality for the self,
So indeed,
The irony of it,
The reality of it,
Is in our earth based reality,
The concept of love,
Can seem fantastical and delusional,
Just not reflective of the lived experience,
Or at least love as we imagine it,
The soft squishy lovely warm fuzzy feeling,
Of course not love in the greatest sense,
Because that's a different philosophical discourse altogether,
Or phenomenon ultimately,
So the soft squishy love,
At the level of where we perceive,
That's the one that is at odds with the reality we sometimes live,
Or the overarching burdensome reality of our existence,
The constant multidimensional conflict and angst,
Intra, inter personally and globally,
Hence why you hear some say love doesn't exist,
The jaded,
The pragmatists,
Who won't be swayed by silly feelings as it were to get a result or their way,
The Machiavellians,
I heard it said that Niccolò Machiavelli is the father of modern politics,
Well it all makes sense then doesn't it,
How things are,

Real Politic they say,
So with 3 days to go,
Where does love fit into all this?
That real love as it were,
Not just the transcendent but the authentic,
The transformational,
The gap between what we imagine,
What we hope for,
And what life is like on the ground so to speak,
Is it a delusional fantasy?
The pursuit of it a fool's errand?
Just a question.

EXISTENCE

With two days left,
The postulation,
Perhaps realisation,
Maybe even conclusion,
Is that,
Well there is the way life is,
Exactly the way it is,
Then there is a choice to make,
Who are you going to be?
What are you going to believe in?
Right up until the end,
Despite all the failures if so,
Setbacks if so,
Betrayals if so,
Disappointments if so,
Challenges if so,
Pain if so,
Your raison detre,
Your focus,
It is said that a founder of one of the famous martial arts systems,
Asked to be buried with his white belt,
Even though he was inspired to create a whole system of human expression,
A unique technique,
A true master,
He knew that you are never done,
Right up until the point of our death here,
Transition as I choose to call it,
There is more to realise,
Discover,
On a true seekers path,
The Upward Road to divinity,
Is endless,
Endlessly Upward,
Challenging and more rewarding,
In this life you leave your legacy,

When you leave and grow till the end,
They are the ones that are remembered and cherished,
The ones who shifted our universal consciousness,
And the ones who loved indefatigably in the quietness of their personal lives,
Whether it was one person they loved tirelessly despite everything till the end,
I have a dream one man once said,
Speaking into the darkness,
Speaking into a dark abyss,
I have a dream,
The words like a boon to a brighter future,
A piercing stab into the heart of darkness,
Then a shot rang out,
From an unknown assailant,
But his work was done,
Because he loved till the end,
Like the martial arts master,
Forever refining the art,
So all there is then is a choice,
All the time,
Within the tempest of human emotion,
Human life,
Like sailors in the heart of the ocean,
Riding giant waves,
And storms whilst the wind blows in all directions,
Capriciously and relentlessly,
Onward toward their destination,
Onward with courage,
Onward,
Onward and upward.

EXISTENCE

With one more day to go,
One finds themselves right at the center of things,
As though at the center of creation,
The center of divinity,
The center of possibility and impossibility,
The center of what could be,
And what might not be,
Seems that is the nature of creation,
And it seems all there is for us is actions to take,
Intentional actions,
Meaningful actions,
Actions inside of some context,
An empowering context,
Some paradigm,
Some belief system,
And that's human existence,
I choose love above all things,
Like a Swiss army knife,
The ultimate tool as it were,
Life's Swiss army knife,
Applicable to offer a solution in every scenario,
An inclusive love at that,
A love that says,
I don't care your colour or creed,
Religion,
Politics,
Gender identity,
Etcetera,
As has been expressed by the highest sages,
And ultimately,
See where it takes me,
Godspeed young man,
Godspeed young soul.

It's finally come,
Day zero,
D day,
The day we meet,
The long wait is over,
And when I finally lay my eyes on you,
It will be like seeing the face of God,
For that's what love is to me,
The face of God,
Smiling,
When I see you,
It will be like a birth,
A rebirth,
Life was this way before,
Now it will be another way,
Better,
Greater,
A deeper knowing,
A deeper connection,
That's love,
The truth,
And even if that experience is only for those brief moments,
For that brief moment,
It'll be more than enough,
It'll be enough to last me the rest of my life time,
Inform the rest of it,
For to have felt true bliss,
Even for a moment,
Is worth everything else there could be on this planet.

EXISTENCE

I am home,
I am home in the place that my soul can rest,
The place where my soul can find peace and tranquillity,
Peace and tranquillity,
That most sacrosanct thing,
The peace and tranquillity even money can't buy,
Who knew it was possible,
I am home,
In your arms,
In your heart,
At peace,
At rest,
What more can a soul ask for,
In this thing we call life,
A privilege and moment,
Worth all the pain and sacrifice to get to,
Thank you for coming into my life,
I thank the universe for bringing you to me,
And I shall take care of you,
And love you,
As such a precious thing should be loved.

Then the excitement comes again,
And you realise it's in the peaks and the troughs that reality is created,
Like the sulci and gyri of the cerebrum,
The peaks and troughs of a wave,
The peaks and valleys of a mountainous relief,
That is the nature of life,
But as with all of it,
When you start at the very bottom,
The baseline level,
The peak is a mighty peak,
At the highest level of excitement,
Accomplishment,
Is bliss,
Contentment,
Jubilation,
So the excitement has come again,
The jubilation,
The jubilation that you are here,
So I hope ours is a life more of jubilation,
As long as we make sure we ensure that,
Within the realms of what we can control,
The rest as ever,
Is in the purview of the heavens,
And to that we surrender,
Surrender in hope,
But surrender.

EXISTENCE

The breath,
The breath,
This mechanism,
This wonder,
The thing that connects us to the beyond,
Not just through the intake of the air we breathe,
This miraculous symbiotic process with our environment,
Our atmosphere,
Miracles beyond miracles,
But just so every day,
The breath that keeps us going,
Gives us life,
The opportunity to be,
To experience life,
Love and all,
The breath,
The miraculous breath,
Connecting us to our inner system,
And the outer world,
Connecting us to everything,
One whole system,
Something so simple,
So common place as to take it for granted,
The breath,
The mighty breath,
Words cannot communicate such wonder,
Even the finest artistry,
The finest word Smith,
Cannot communicate this level of majesty,
The breath,
The universal design of it all,
Summed up in one phenomenon,
The love and intention to make all this possible,
Is enough to humble the soul,
When you see,
When you truly see,

The breath,
The gateway,
The access,
To each lived moment,
To the next moment of life.
Hence, then,
It becomes conclusively apparent,
If it wasn't before,
Despite repetition after repetition,
Highest teacher after highest teacher,
Guru after guru,
Enlightened to enlightened,
Through the ages,
The generations,
That love is the way,
The pursuit of it,
The truest pursuit of love,
Of the purest love,
The love that brings you through the darkness,
The love where there is a bright luminescence at the end of the toil,
The most beautiful sunrise,
So then,
It's not that you won't get very lost,
Or you won't be in the darkest cave at times,
The darkest times,
Or maybe in the most pain you could ever imagine,
Come as close as possible to the end,
Perhaps right to the ledge,
The edge,
It's that if love is the rock,
The cornerstone,
The anchor,
The quest,
You will step back from the ledge,
Make your way through the cave,
And in time,

EXISTENCE

I promise you,
You will see even brighter suns,
Brighter, brighter suns,
So bright that it's perhaps unbelievably dazzling,
For it seems self-evident,
That things mean more,
If the struggle has been greatest,
The famine,
The pain,
And also it's to take a leap of faith,
That even if you die in what you thought was pain,
I assure you too that ultimately,
In the highest dimensions,
At the highest level,
The universe is beautifully just.

I never knew love could be like this,
I never knew life could be like this,
See,
You must see,
That for decades,
I hated existence,
Even the love that was there,
I didn't see it,
I didn't even love myself,
I called myself a misanthrope,
I was proud that I knew the word,
I believed it described me perfectly,
I discovered it reading Mark Twain,
So it had more veracity,
Someone as venerated as him,
I share some of his feelings,
Or what he must have felt at some point,
So yes,
I'm a misanthrope,
And proud,
And convicted in my misanthropic world view,
And justified,
Vindicated every time I turned on the news,
Or scrolled through social media in some ways,
The nasty comments,
The horrible videos,
And of course the forever bickering politicians,
Mastering the art of recrimination,
In some instances lies and subterfuge,
And some cases downright oppression,
Murder,
So yes,
I believed,
The world is a terrible place,
Humans are terrible,
Life is terrible,

EXISTENCE

Terrible and horrible,
But the seed of love that had always been planted in me by those who loved me persisted,
And today it has finally germinated,
Sprung forth from the earth,
Into the fresh air of life and new opportunity,
Into the sun rays of hope,
Today I have learnt that true love is the ultimate redeemer,
That yes as the sages have said,
That age old pithy statement says,
Love conquers all,
All I will say though,
Is make sure its true love,
For some may manipulate your desire to love and make you hate,
Make you kill,
Exploit you,
Cause division,
The truest path of love,
Only unites,
Brings solutions,
And ultimately brings harmony,
A new space for beauty to be possible,
Even where it might not have been today,
I truly know this today,
And I will never go back,
Today the eyes have seen,
What they never can unsee,
The soul has learnt,
What it can never unlearn,
Praise the heavens,
Praise the universe,
A quest is only a true quest when there's been struggle,
But what is worth struggling for which is good,
Is truly worth it,
Choose wisely,
I chose love.

Your life,
Is predominantly shaped,
When you are at your weakest,
And when you are at your strongest,
When you are at your weakest,
It's perhaps when life has brought you to your knees,
And when you are at your strongest is when you are full of vigour and power,
Self-determining,
So I say today,
Always choose love when you are at your weakest and when you are at your strongest,
When you are at your weakest,
Use love as a beacon to guide you back on the right track,
The Universe's direction and road map,
For when you are at your weakest,
That's when the felonious whispers come in,
Those whispers that could kill, misguide and destroy you,
And maybe those around you,
Those whispers that rob you of strength,
More so,
If you don't choose love,
When you are strong,
Well the world you create can be an ugly one,
Choose love,
Choose love,
Choose love,
Always.

EXISTENCE

Your love is like an un blossomed flower,
A slow blooming flower,
Cocooned in its sepal,
Guarded,
Secretive,
Unwilling to unfurl,
Let go,
Open and expose your petals,
Your inner beauty,
Your inner workings,
Your inner sanctum,
Indeed, it's good to value your inner sanctum,
To guard your inner sanctum,
Trust is won over time.

A heart's that's been broken can be impatient,
Looking to be proved right,
Prove,
Prove already that you're here to hurt me,
Prove,
Prove already that this love won't last,
Prove,
Prove already that you're just like the others,
Or someone who hurt the heart before,
Hurry up and prove it,
The broken heart says,
So it can clam up,
Close again,
Lift up the barriers,
Close like a Venus fly trap,
With great rapidity,
Bring up the draw bridge,
So it's shielded from the pain,
It takes a brave one to love again,
The truly brave to let someone in again,
Who could break your heart into a million pieces again,
But of course,
Love is for the brave,
Who told you it wasn't.

EXISTENCE

Once the commitment is made,
Then it's all about trust,
It becomes all about trust,
But to commit in love,
Is in a way,
Not just in a way,
It's tantamount to putting your life in someone else's hands,
That's why if that trust is broken,
That bond is broken,
Especially a really strong and deep one,
It feels like a loss,
A death,
The death of all those projected expectations and ideals,
The death of the dreams,
The death of the bond,
The death of the trust,
A spiritual death,
That can feel like a physical death,
And so it is,
The lover's curse,
The true lover's curse,
To risk it all,
In the pursuit of joy and happiness,
No wonder why some,
When they find themselves with someone not worth their trust,
Not worth their commitment ,
They just can't let go,
Who can let go of these deep seated fantasies we create when we fall in love?
For love can be like a fantasy against the seemingly true back drop of reality,
So who would want to step out of that?
Might as well keep the dream going,
Avoid the hurt of facing letting go,
Letting go of the deep penetrative emotions that have been set,
Who can judge?

For ultimately everything is a lesson in the end anyway,
So then,
All we can hope for,
Is that those we fall in love with,
Love us as much as we love them,
Care for us as much as we care for them,
Want the best for us,
As much as we want the best for them,
Value us,
As much as we value them,
Are not in it for themselves,
Not in it only for what they can get out of the commitment,
The relationship,
See things both ways,
Not just their way,
Are we willing to give,
Not just take,
Willing to give,
Not just receive,
Then that's the proper kind of love,
And that's a blessing in this life of ours.

EXISTENCE

The person you love,
Or the person who loves you,
Should empower you,
See the greatness in you,
More than you see it in yourself,
Want what's best for you,
More than you want it for yourself,
See the good qualities in you,
That you didn't even know existed,
Admire you in a way,
That you have never been admired,
And when you're with the one that truly loves you,
Your greatest self naturally comes out,
Now that's sweet love.

The thing about love,
That iridescent love,
That shimmers and sparkles,
It is timeless,
In the near term,
And in the long term,
That's why you can fall deeply in love really quickly,
And that's why those who truly love each other,
Love each other beyond death,
You can fall in love so quickly,
And get so close to someone,
That it can feel like you've known them forever,
Even though by how we measure time,
It's not chronologically consistent,
But that can also speak to the deepest dimensions of reality,
The deepest aspects of truth,
But that's for another time,
However,
At this time,
Just to speak to the all-consuming power of love,
The all-conquering,
Conquering time,
And death,
Conquering time and death,
What a thing to believe in,
And better yet a good thing,
So love can bend time,
Create experiences that feel outside of our time,
But even more so,
Keep us connected,
When one has left the world of flesh and form,
And the other remains,
Such a thought,
Brings tears to the eyes,
But good tears,
Healing tears,
Calming tears,
Transcendent tears.

EXISTENCE

The thing about love,
The deepest love,
When you are sitting above it all,
Is that you can love everything,
The chaos,
The madness,
Everything,
See,
Love generates understanding,
It is an inclusive phenomenon,
A uniting phenomenon,
Hate generates confusion and discord,
It is a separating phenomenon,
A dismembering phenomenon,
When you love,
You see,
And for us humans,
When you love,
You see as clearly as we possibly can,
And when you're loving from the highest place,
You see the beauty of it all,
Hence, for myself,
As a poet,
To have loved for five years and left our plain,
Is better than,
Having hated for ninety five years then left this plain,
For in those five years,
You would have seen more,
About the true meaning of this whole thing,
This complex tapestry we call life,
Than ninety five whole years of hate.

When you reach the pinnacle of observation,
Of love and wisdom,
Even if it's just an epiphany,
In a moment,
It becomes even as much as hilarious,
Or perhaps pitiful,
To observe,
Or hear spiteful, hateful or prejudiced words come out of someone,
Oh, if only you could see blind man,
Blind person,
What your spiritual blindness shields you from.

EXISTENCE

And it is said,
If you reach enlightenment,
Or when you reach enlightenment,
So it goes,
Chop wood,
Enlightenment,
Chop wood,
Euphoria is short lived,
The pinnacle of anything is a moment in time,
Only a passing period,
An entry point,
A beginning,
An insight,
A deeper insight,
A state change,
But the system always goes back to a resting state,
Homogenises,
Acclimatises,
Otherwise, it burns itself out,
The system always goes back to center,
To rest,
Homeostasis,
So that the journey continues,
Continues under a new normal perhaps,
It might even retrograde or regress for a while,
But the journey always continues,
The thing is the journey,
The journey,
The journey,
So even in love,
It's not going to feel good all the time,
Be clear all the time,
Be euphoric all the time,
And that's probably the biggest pitfall for most,
That when the height of elation has subsided,
And the headwinds are strong ,

And it's perhaps not enjoyable,
Or hard work,
Even confusing,
Then perhaps you want to retreat,
So in a reciprocating love,
It's the journey,
Because you don't stop chopping wood,
Else there is no fire to keep you warm,
Chop wood,
Enlightenment,
Chop wood.

EXISTENCE

And then it's the biggest realisation of all,
The grandest realisation,
The big daddy,
The granddaddy,
That in all seriousness,
That to love,
You must lead by example,
You must lead,
You must lead,
And to lead,
Is to lead when it's hardest,
For our life is hard,
We wish it wasn't,
But it is,
But if you master love,
Being powered by love,
Then in a perfect world it could become easier,
And the perfect world,
Would be possible,
If everyone was doing the same,
To really love,
You have to be an example of love,
Not in theory,
In action,
Not to say one thing,
Then do the other,
Profess one thing,
Then do the other,
And when you are being given by love,
Then the world is a completely different place,
And clearly our life is hard,
Because most of us do not do this,
If not all of us,
Or we do so narrowly,
So it's been said before,
And it will be said again here,

For what's good and right,
In a world as complex as ours,
Perhaps cannot be said enough,
Perhaps until it doesn't need to be said anymore,

EXISTENCE

Then,
When you truly love,
You realise,
It's not their ignorance you need to conquer,
Their malice,
Or hatred,
It's yours.

The irony about love,
And loving,
Is the pain it can cause,
The pain of loss,
The loss of it,
The thing you loved,
Whatever it is,
Some people can't recover from the loss,
In truth,
Some losses are unbearable,
Perhaps all losses,
Yet,
One can say,
The best approach contrary to what so many do,
Which is focus on the loss,
The pain,
The wrongs or the wrong that was done to you,
Live in anger,
Seek vengeance,
Fan the fans of hatred,
Carry so much resentment,
That perhaps you carry it to your next incarnation,
The best approach is instead to focus on the lessons,
See everything as a lesson,
An upward lesson,
Grounded perhaps in the belief and realisation that,
We are spiritual beings having an earthly existence,
All that we go through,
Is attached to a greater purpose,
And always track that through all the pain and confusion,
Then to say that,
Even the wide expanse of human history,
And all that we have done to ourselves and each other,
Is an evolutionary path of transformation,
So then there is no pain, misery, injustice,
Betrayal and all the rest of it,

EXISTENCE

I mean, of course there is,
But the point is,
What do we learn from the opportunity of it all,
From the event of it all,
From the eventuality of it all.

In the end,
One of the true super powers of love,
Is that it inspires hope,
It allows you to teleport to a future of possibility,
Through the mire and miasma of your current circumstances,
Hope through the darkest and most confusing times,
It allows you to always imagine the possibility,
The possibility of a better tomorrow.

EXISTENCE

The insanity of it all,
In life and in love,
Is what we fight over,
Can be the smallest misunderstandings,
Incandescent blazing rows,
Anger and resentment,
Over the smallest things,
A miscommunication,
A small omission,
A small mistake,
And once the battle lines are drawn,
Sometimes there is no going back,
Like two bulls locked in battle,
Now it's just a battle to the end,
A battle for dominance and superiority,
What it was even about,
Who knows,
Who cares,
And for this,
So much is lost,
It surely is a bit insane,
That's why the peaceful path,
Is the only path,
For whatever you are fighting or killing for,
It's never justified,
Not truly,
No matter what St Thomas Aquinas said.

Polaris,
My North star,
I can't get lost,
Because you stay steady and true,
Your love is consistent,
Unflinching,
So as I search and search in the darkness,
All I must do is raise my head up,
And you are there,
And I'll surely find my way home.

EXISTENCE

The love and devotion,
Of someone special,
Special to you,
That's one of the greatest privileges of human existence,
One of the true wonders of the universe,
The unique privilege of being alive,
To find it,
Sacrosanct.

My heart flutters,
My heart skips a beat,
Part in disbelief ,
How such a creature,
Of such immense beauty,
Could appear my life,
And choose me,
And choose to be by my side,
Such immense beauty,
Inside and out,
I thank the heavens,
For sometimes it rains,
Thunderstorms,
And some days are beautiful radiant sunshine,
You are such days.

EXISTENCE

Your beauty is transfixing,
Haunting,
Captivating,
The contours of your face,
Moulded to perfection by the deliberate very hand of the creator,
Or whether it's the expansive, refining and remodelling evolutionary process of time,
Which moulded your contours to perfection,
Elegantly and marvellously,
For you spawned flawlessly,
Your beautiful big brown eyes,
Seductive and innocent,
The sweetness of a true woman,
Who knows who and what she is,
Your lips,
If lips could be described as voluptuous,
Yours would be,
Full and perfect,
Just like you,
They say beauty lies in the eye of the beholder,
But I think with you,
All will agree,
Blessed you are with such beauty,
And privileged I am to be your chosen one.

Musings upon musings on love,
Musings upon musings on love,
Why not?
Musings upon musings on love.

EXISTENCE

For love to work,
It can only be both ways,
Both ways,
All ways.

Your love,
Was sent to me from the ancestral plains,
It was sent to me,
From my ancestors,
For they live in the plain,
Where all is clear,
And they knew exactly what I needed,
I needed you,
Your words,
Your energy,
Your essence,
Your spirit,
Your intentions,
Align with mine,
You illuminate my dark shadows,
Such that even disagreement,
Is an access to clarity,
And I am refined,
Enhanced,
Augmented,
As a result,
The wisdom of my forebears,
All that they know about what life is,
What it should be,
From their combined experiences,
Through time,
Reside in you,
Reside in us,
This is love,
This is true love.

EXISTENCE

In a world full of so much hurt and pain,
Malice and ignorance,
It can confuse the soul,
Confuse the senses,
Especially when one has suffered,
Or has been hurt before,
Can I afford to let go again?
Trust again?
Let someone in?
Let love in?
Truly in?
To take a chance,
Such that I'm vulnerable,
Again,
In the hands of the other,
In the hands of others,
Heartbreak is such a devastating thing,
Betrayal,
Brutality,
Injustice,
We walk around with a deep sense of distrust,
To an extent,
And some to a great extent,
As individuals,
As groups,
So much hurt,
So much pain,
That some don't even believe in love,
So what is required?
Courage,
And faith,
Belief,
Time and time again,
Despite it all,
All the disappointments,
The pain,

Confusion and hurt,
What's required,
Is a spirit that never gives up,
A spirit that looks to hope,
Otherwise all that's left if not,
Is to resign to the darkness,
So I choose to let love in,
Choose to trust,
Choose to trust,
Choose to let love in.

EXISTENCE

The hardest thing,
Is letting go,
Can be letting go,
All those attachments,
Dreams and fantasies that drive us,
The connection we had,
Our idealism,
Fixed ideas,
Fixed expectations,
Disappointments,
Forgiving,
Forgetting,
Maybe not forgiving or forgetting,
But moving on,
Moving on from the past,
Healing,
Creating new space,
Space for something new.

You say you are my star,
Inkanyezi yakho,
My beautiful star,
You've said this,
Not me,
But I agree,
Yes,
Yes you are,
My beautiful star.

EXISTENCE

It is purported,
That modern humans,
Sapiens,
Have existed,
For approximately three hundred thousand years,
As a species,
By those who know such things,
Or claim to know,
We have come from the palaeolithic period apparently,
Where we just manipulated stones,
Today we manipulate atoms,
Evolution is an undeniable phenomenon,
No matter what you believe,
So, certainly humanity is evolving,
Socially,
Politically,
Technologically,
And hopefully spiritually,
For our sense of justice and accountability,
Has rapidly progressed in recent history,
We have contrived ourselves to be bound by rules as a species that we didn't have before,
As one of the greatest souls of the last century said,
He reminded us,
Indeed he told us,
That the moral arch of the universe is long,
And it bends towards justice,
Hence, perhaps the moral arch of love is long,
So then perhaps humanity is evolving towards love,
Perhaps.

To love in the face of hatred,
To love in the face of no agreement,
To love in the face of ignorance,
To love in face of obstinance,
To love in the face of intransigence,
To love in the face of malice,
To love in the midst of confusion,
To love where there is no love,
To love all that seems putrid,
To love even those who will only love themselves.

EXISTENCE

Love,
True love,
Knows no barriers,
No borders,
No boundaries,
Not bound by distance,
Not bound by time,
Hence,
True love is transcendent,
True love is in transcendence,
Through all barriers.

Love is acceptance,
Acceptance of everything,
Exactly as it is,
Then when you accept,
You love,
You love even more,
And build with love,
And choose good,
And when you choose good,
Your soul will always be at peace.

EXISTENCE

Love,
True love is seeing the beauty of it all,
From the darkest shadows,
To the most illuminated spaces,
The symmetry,
The Synergy,
Seeing the intrinsic value of the animate,
The inanimate,
The sentient,
The supposed insentient,
All of it,
The grand majestic picture,
Then sit at the top,
The very tip of understanding and appreciation,
And enjoy and view it all,
As it plays out,
Like the most beautiful story ever told,
The most beautiful story,
Life,
Love.

At the center of knowing,
At the center of love,
Is the ultimate knowledge that,
Our existence,
Has nothing to do with all these externalities we obsess about,
Myriad they are,
At the center of knowing,
At the center of love,
Our existence has nothing to do with any of that.

EXISTENCE

Perhaps like every great tale,
Full of trials and tribulations,
Our hero,
Our protagonist,
You,
Is plagued by all these challenges,
But our heroes always have a fundamental belief in something,
Something good,
And like every great tale,
It has a beginning, a middle and an end,
And if you knew everything about it,
Every twist and turn,
Every plot twist,
Well ultimately,
There would be no point listening to the tale,
Such is life,
It has a beginning, a middle and an end,
With many plot twists,
And each one of us,
The hero in the tale,
The hero in the play,
And if we knew all that was going to happen,
Well there would be no meaning,
No growth,
The meaning,
Well that's a transcendent phenomenon,
The growth ,
Well that's in overcoming adversity positively,
That has material effect in this life,
And too, the end is a transcendent phenomenon,
But the best meaning and most meaningful growth,
Is found by having love as the central principle.

The curiosity,
Is that,
We think we are more,
Better,
Advanced,
But the truth is,
We are the same,
As those untamed beasts in the deepest jungle,
Predators and prey,
Prey and predators,
Territorial,
Savage,
Brutal,
Killers,
In our own human jungle,
Our only difference,
Perhaps advantage,
Maybe freedom,
Is that we can choose,
To choose love,
We can choose to be loving,
Tame the wild untamed beast,
We can choose.

EXISTENCE

Love heals

A lover said to his love,
Thank you for bringing love back into my broken heart,
And she replied,
Always,
You deserve a love greater than what I can give you,
Then she went on to say,
Please accept the meagre love that my human heart can give,
How beautiful is that?
That's what love does,
That's what love elicits,
How much more beautiful is that?
How much better is that than what hate, cruelty and torture can elicit?
Enmity?
Which is the better path?
It seems pretty clear to me.
What is better to fight and strive for?
What is better to believe in?

EXISTENCE

Love can embrace all,
Envelope all,
In a warm embrace,
Hate can burn everything to the ground,
Everything,
Till there is nothing left,
But smouldering cinders,
And even then,
It won't be content,
It will seek more to destroy,
Like a vacuum,
A black hole,
Voraciously sucking everything in,
Into permanent oblivion,
Uncaring,
Insatiable,
Yet love is caring,
Love,
True love embraces all.

Judgement,
Is in the way of love,
Love and understanding,
Then maybe peace.

EXISTENCE

One day,
I saw a soldier,
Dressed in the uniform of my enemy,
The full regalia,
With pride he strode,
A uniform that has killed so many of my people,
And I could be any human on this planet,
So my instinct was to hate him,
I didn't want to talk to him,
Even though I had to,
But I realised,
I'm on a quest to discover love,
The true meaning of love,
How do you love someone,
Who has killed you for centuries,
How do you love someone,
Trained to kill you,
Even trained to hate you,
So in that moment,
I realised how truly complex this life of ours is,
Yet I'm on a mission to discover love,
By any means necessary,
So I searched,
Searched my consciousness here and beyond,
And I dug deep,
Past my immediate anger,
Hatred and prejudice,
And I discovered that,
I am him,
And he is me,
For me to be,
He has to be,
For my purpose and life to have meaning,
To be someone searching for love and peace in this world,
He has to be a trained soldier,
Trained to hurt and kill,

Then something incredible happened,
When I got past me,
I then saw him,
In his body,
Looking withered and frail,
Probably seen some of the ugliest things still haunting his mind to this day,
Maybe,
Probably have been made to do things that hurt his conscience,
Killed his conscience,
Cut him off in this life from the totality of love,
I saw his amputated finger,
I then saw that he too is human,
He too is a victim of cruelty and ignorance,
Then I saw that what is, is,
And what will be,
Will be,
I can only do what I can do,
And he can only be who he is meant to be,
Then we go into the ground,
Or we become ash,
And what was me,
And what was him goes somewhere else,
I believe somewhere very beautiful,
Then I sighed a sigh of relief,
And I told myself,
That my friend,
It is all beautiful,
It's beautiful if you believe in love.

EXISTENCE

There must be love in the world,
For some dedicate their lives to love and care,
Caring for little children,
Caring for the weak,
Yes some kill,
Some kill little children,
But others heal,
The Dichotic Dilemma.

Love has risen again,
Like the return of a great messiah,
A long awaited messiah,
Love has risen again,
Like the sunrise at dawn,
Love has risen again,
Like spring time after a long winter,
New possibilities are arising,
Like the new shoots of spring,
New life,
New life,
Love has risen again,
Like the great deliverer,
A great conqueror,
Conquering darkness and sadness,
Love has risen again,
Like a mighty King,
Ready to rule over his Kingdom with justice and wisdom,
Love has risen again,
Like a loving God,
Ready to forgive all those who have sinned,
And heal all wounds and pain,
So that there may be at least one day of perfect beauty for humanity,
Love has risen again in my heart,
For once I believed,
But hurt, pain, confusion and suffering had come and robbed me of my belief,
And all there was,
Was darkness,
The blackest night,
But today,
Finally,
Love has risen again,
Love has returned,
And my heart believes again,
My faith is restored,

EXISTENCE

My hope that had become as sparse as vegetation in the most arid desert,
Is now like the most verdant forest,
Full of greenery and beauty,
Or like a powerful exploding volcano,
Irrepressible,
Awesome,
Thanks to the miraculous touch of a loving hand,
Thanks to the gift of actually genuinely being loved,
By someone who not so long ago was a stranger,
Yet now,
The connection is truly profound,
They say a stranger is a friend you haven't met yet,
A stranger indeed is a friend you haven't met yet.

There is beauty here,
There is,
So much beauty.

EXISTENCE

Love is getting present to the impossible,
For one day I said,
I did not want children,
The world is an ugly place,
But today I can't imagine the world without them,
And my life is not ugly,
But infinitely more beautiful for having them in it.

Even if the raging flames of infatuation die down,
Or the peak of attraction and affection,
Wains for a bit,
That's fine too,
Because you don't always want to be in front of a raging fire,
Sometimes it's comfortable just to be in front of the cooling embers,
The lesson and point being,
You can always reignite the flame.

EXISTENCE

I hope you have enjoyed the book and the poems, musing on the idea and phenomenon of love. Love is my belief system and so that's all I'm trying to spread. Just a bit more love in the world. However, often times I think people misunderstand love and see it as a weakness, but I see it as a strength. A driving force to overcome all and any challenges and more so if our collective species was powered by love inside of a singular understanding. Well then that's truly hypothetical conjecture.

So, I'll leave it there. However, just to conclude by saying, hate and all of that really is in the way. The most deepened appreciation of love is the quantum leap. Truly loving is much harder than hating. Hating is easy. It takes no effort. No imagination and it's ultimately lazy and corrosive. To love you must dig deep, imagine, sacrifice, learn, grow, care. Care outside of yourself sometimes. I suppose I am labouring the point now.

Godspeed human race.

The thing about darkness is if it too thinks it's the light then it doesn't know it's the dark.

EXISTENCE

The day the nuclear bombs fell,
And humanity was eviscerated from the planet,
Eviscerated itself from existence on this planet,
The cockroaches celebrated,
Finally,
They are gone,
How dare they call us pests,
They killed us en masse,
On sight,
With their pesticides,
And their slippers,
Hooray,
The tyranny of the human race is at an end,
How dare they call us pests,
We were here aeons before them,
They were the true pests,
The carnage they brought in such a short space of time,
In many ways unbalanced ecosystems,
Caused species extinctions,
And we are the pests?
We pre date the dinosaurs they loved so much,
We are the true custodians of this planet,
And the rest of the flora and fauna on the planet heard the cockroaches and joined them in celebration,
And they all called an amnesty towards each other,
To have one day of celebration,
To celebrate the end of the scourge of the human race,
Who were so barbaric,
They built the most destructive weapons and ended their own civilisation,
And we were the so called lesser beings on the planet,
Less intelligent,
The irony,
Oh the irony,
Hooray to the end of the human race the cockroaches said,
They were given everything by God,

The Universe,
But they just couldn't get along,
They admired war and conflict so much,
Judged each other so harshly,
Cared for their so called own kind,
When they were all human,
What dumb beasts,
And the universe didn't mind either,
When humanity killed itself,
Because all the wonders of the universe did not cease when humanity ceased.

www.ingramcontent.com/pod-product-compliance
Lightning Source LLC
LaVergne TN
LVHW091556060526
838200LV00036B/860